For my babies who are always questioning everything: Noah, Milo, Zen and Lotus, and for Elijah McClain 🎻

www.theenglishschoolhouse.com

Copyright © 2021 by Dr. Tamara Pizzoli

All rights reserved. This book or any portion thereof may not be reproduced or used in any manner whatsoever without the express written permission of the author except for the use of brief quotations in a book review. This is a work of fiction. Names, characters, places, and incidents are a product of the author's imagination. Any resemblance to actual persons, events, or locales is entirely coincidental.

ISBN: 978-1-955130-05-9

Elijah Everett, Kid Principal

By Dr. Tamara Pizzoli

Illustrated by Tommaso Chiarolini

If you let the teachers and staff at McPherson Elementary tell it, Elijah Everett was a problem child and a complete bother.

All the students knew just what the adults thought about Elijah.

As far as the teachers were concerned, Elijah had absolutely no interest in following rules, directives, or even suggestions.

Elijah's teachers labeled him with all sorts of unfavorable adjectives, like "difficult".

The cafeteria ladies rolled their eyes when they saw him coming.

The gym teacher threatened to retire early when Elijah showed up to class.

And the Principal, Ms. Meyer, secretly wished Elijah would just transfer to another school.

There were tall tales about Elijah that traveled around the school with lightning speed and complete inaccuracy.

No one bothered to verify if they were actually true.

Early one Monday morning, an announcement was made from the Principal's office.

"In celebration of Principal's week, a raffle will be held to decide which lucky student will get to be Principal for a week! You heard right! One of you pupils will swap spots with Principal Meyer for five whole school days!"

Every classroom, hallway, and even restroom at McPherson Elementary was buzzing with excitement. There wasn't a student from kindergarten to fifth grade who didn't want a shot at being Principal for a week. They all submitted their names for consideration.

Enter to be Principal for the Week Here!

For Office use only

The next morning, Principal Meyer reached her hand inside of a jar that contained the names of over five hundred children.

She pulled out a folded slip of paper and clutched it tightly. "Students," she began, "I'm pleased to announce that your Principal for the entirety of next week will be..."

There was a long pause followed by an audible gulp.

The entire school sat stunned, except for Elijah, who stepped into his new role almost immediately. He pulled a small rectangular stack from his pocket and began passing out his business cards to both friends and faculty.

The following Monday rolled around soon enough. Principal Elijah was the first person to arrive at McPherson Elementary School. He was dressed for success and ready to work. Elijah greeted each pupil as they filed in the front door with either a high-five or a handshake.

Right away, Elijah implemented new routines and initiatives schoolwide. The school day began with a morning snack and a classroom chat, followed by meditation.

Quizzes and tests were immediately replaced with casual conversations to check for learning.
The curriculum, Principal Elijah announced, would consist of students choosing what they wanted to learn.

Recess was extended from fifteen minutes to one full hour. Principal Elijah corralled the cafeteria staff and spearheaded much needed improvements to the school's breakfast and lunch menu.

A suggestion box was added to the school's entrance, and Principal Elijah read the comments and critiques with great attention each evening.

Two massage therapists were hired for the teacher's lounge.

By the end of the week, Principal Meyer had to admit the school was running like a well-oiled machine. To boot, she had never seen so many students smiling and enjoying their time at school.

When the clock struck 3 pm on Friday afternoon, the entire student body along with the faculty and staff gave Principal Elijah much deserved praise for a job well done.

The next Monday, Elijah returned to his regular seat as a fifth grade student...with a few privileges.

Made in the USA
Columbia, SC
08 April 2025